T0303736

# More Praise for
# *Wallflower*

"Peter Bullen constructs seemingly simple scenarios and creates the occasion for hilarious and masterfully crafted encounters with endearing speakers and their unassuming beloved. In this space, he presents the ruminations of someone who always overthinks the equation of his subjects— their possible rejections and dismissals—often ending in a more lucid understanding of self and the bewildering unknown of the other. Everything is sincere and without a shred of sentimentality. In this collection, we are guided on a tour of love, humor, self-doubt, and natural revelation that any reader finds most satisfying in the very best kind of fiction."

– **TRACEY KNAPP**, author of *Mouth*,
winner of the 2014 42 Miles Press Poetry Award

# Wallflower

Peter Thomas Bullen

# NOMADIC PRESS

**OAKLAND**
111 FAIRMOUNT AVENUE
OAKLAND, CA 94611

**BROOKLYN**
475 KENT AVENUE #302
BROOKLYN, NY 11249

WWW.NOMADICPRESS.ORG

**MASTHEAD**

*FOUNDING AND MANAGING EDITOR*
J. K. FOWLER

*ASSOCIATE EDITOR*
MICHAELA MULLIN

*DESIGN*
J. K. FOWLER

**MISSION STATEMENT**

Through publications, events, and active community participation, Nomadic Press collectively weaves together platforms for intentionally marginalized voices to take their rightful place within the world of the written and spoken word. Through its limited means, we are simply attempting to help right the centuries' old violence and silencing that should never have occurred in the first place and build alliances and community partnerships with others who share a collective vision for a future far better than today.

**SUBMISSIONS**

Nomadic Press wholeheartedly accepts unsolicited book manuscripts. To submit your work, please visit www.nomadicpress.org/submissions

**DISTRIBUTION**

Orders by trade bookstores and wholesalers:
Small Press Distribution,
1341 Seventh Street
Berkeley, CA 94701
spd@spdbooks.org
(510) 524-1668 / (800) 869-7553

## Wallflower

This book was made possible by a loving community of chosen family and friends, old and new.

For author questions or to book a reading at your bookstore, university/school, or alternative establishment, please send an email to info@nomadicpress.org.

Cover artwork by Arthur Johnstone and Livien Yin. Author portrait by Arthur Johnstone.

Published by Nomadic Press, 111 Fairmount Avenue, Oakland, CA 94611

Second printing, 2020

LIBRARY OF CONGRESS CATALOGING-IN-PUBLICATION DATA

Thomas Bullen, Peter 1952 –
Title: *Wallflower*
P. CM.
Summary: These are stories of desire, identity, folly, tenderness, and maybe even hope. Hapless males with heart, but not exactly gumption, walk into situations with strong women with ideas on what to do with hapless males. Men not necessarily finding out, women not all the way certain  . . . beauty's uninterpretable call; an invisible ear pressed to a non-existent wall . . . love stories in other words.

[1. FICTION. 2. LOVE. 3. HUMOR. 4. AMERICAN GENERAL.] I. III. TITLE.

LIBRARY OF CONGRESS CONTROL NUMBER: 2016953744

ISBN: 978-0-9981348-1-9

# Wallflower

Peter Thomas Bullen

**NOMADIC
PRESS**

*for Alison*

# CONTENTS

1 HEARTH AND HOME

3 THE READING

8 ADMIRATION

14 UNWISE

19 TAKE TWO

25 A DATE

30 MIXED FORMULA

34 WHO?

37 POETRY

39 UNGLUED

43 DINNER

46 FEAR OF POETS

48 AUTHOR

50 LOVERS

53 INCIDENT

57 ROOM

# HEARTH AND HOME

**WHEN I GOT HOME** from work, my wife informed me that she'd seen a man she didn't know stepping out of our shower fully clothed. I was tired and wanted to tell my wife how fatigued I felt. Clearly it was not a good time to do so. Even in my exhausted condition, I knew to be grateful that my wife had not seen a naked man emerge from our shower. But a naked man exiting a shower does come with certain advantages. For instance, he would surely reach for a towel. A man who takes a shower with his clothes on is something of a rebel and could not be counted on to behave in thoughtful and considerate ways. On his way out of the house, he would have strolled through our living room. An alarming thought. Our living room contained a rare and very delicate Persian carpet. What if the showering intruder had walked over it, sat on it, laid down on it even, all of which seemed plausible from a drenched deviant. I wanted to check the carpet immediately, run upstairs to my office, and Google "Persian carpets/water damage." I held myself back. It was a typical moment in my marriage, this squashing of my true desire, my real wish, knowing that to share it openly with my wife would reveal something dreadful about my character. My wife, with a look of consternation passing over her freckled face, waited patiently for my response. I remembered then how madly I'd loved her, how I had wanted to devour her, how I'd worshipped every last freckle on her body. But time had passed and the ugly truth, which I had a feeling she could sense, was that I was thinking less about the dangers posed by the intruder and more about the impact his dripping self may have had on our carpet. Without saying anything, it was obvious to both of us that our marriage was over.

After our separation, I left the law firm with its frenzied pace and constant crisis management. Feeling rested at last, I took up interior design, working with a small, select group of clients who appreciated my rarefied esthetic. My new life had an air of leisure and fulfillment about it until I developed a peculiar habit that I could not explain or resist. Once a month on Sundays, I rented a Cadillac with tinted windows and drove to my wife's house, the one we'd lived and loved in together. I was struck by how little nostalgia, how little feeling, I had as I cruised by. Last Sunday changed all that. Through the car's darkened windows, I saw my wife on the front lawn. It was as if I was seeing her for the first time. She was ravishing. By her side sat an enormous bucket, and across from her a handsome man lounged in a silver grey three-piece suit. My wife lifted up the bucket, stood, and with a perfect mix of ferocity and pleasure proceeded to empty the water-filled bucket over his head. He took her in his arms. She shrieked with joy.

I've not been the same since.

# THE READING

**I'D BEEN SENT.** As if I was a person in need of being sent someplace other than where I was. Where I was was with a woman I thought needed me. It's not like she ever said she needed me. What she said was, "Come home with me." She only said it once. It didn't bear repeating, or she couldn't bear to repeat it; it comes to much the same. I thought maybe I was a writer. She thought I was a person in need of advice. She said to go see this guy Jack read at the bookstore. "He's a writer," she said in a tone that implied maybe I wasn't.

The bookstore is jam-packed. Just the fact that there is a bookstore is surprising; that it's filled with people adds to my surprise, and my irritation. One more example of excited people gathered to see someone who is not me. Like I need more examples. There are far more women than men. I figure this Jack guy is one of those handsome writers. "Fucking handsome writer," I mutter to myself, although no one has yet appeared. Many in the crowd seem to know each other. There is the whisper of anticipation. Hate that.

A lady in a floral blouse, black pants, and masculine-looking shoes arrives at the podium. First thing that pops into my head: *if she's going to wear shoes like that, why not dispense with the flowery top? Where's the consistency?* I'm angry with everyone. You can be pissed off at a literary reading in exactly the same way you can be pissed off in stop-and-go traffic. I keep making discoveries like this. It is not uplifting. The woman starts gabbing about the wonders of this Jack guy, telling a story of being at a workshop of his where he forbade her to leave until she put down on paper her real and true feelings. Feelings about what, she doesn't go into, and for that small mercy I am grateful. The whole thing sounds sexual to me, like he's the literary dungeon master and she's the enslaved wench clutching her Moleskine. That might just be my weird perspective. I'd like to be free of weird perspectives, but, in a way, they're the only ones I have. She goes on to explain how the restriction was in force for twenty-four hours, and how she was not allowed to leave the room until the task was accomplished. Jack watched over her even when nature called. It just gets more and more sexual sounding to me, and I start to expect gasps from the audience, but everyone seems enthralled, in the way scholarly people are enthralled, not in the way titillated people are enthralled, which has a whole different vibe. I start to think of the scenario she's describing as a type of imprisonment for art, with an arousing subtext I don't altogether understand but which is starting to arouse me, and that totally changes my attitude.

I feel I've been converted.

I'm thinking like, lock me up and throw away the key until I produce something resembling art. Maybe that's why the bookstore is packed to the rafters; the great jailor of aspiring writers is here in the flesh. So now I start to wish he'd capture me, which shows how far you can come in terms of mood change in a short period of time. I totally forgive the lady's poor sense of style and remember that I'm no fashion model myself. I too kind of want to follow her to the bathroom until she's produced another piece of authentic prose, but before I can take those thoughts further a new woman comes out to replace the one in men's shoes. This new woman is a whole other thing. She's like biker mama/Beat poet/Latin teacher all in one. How is that possible, you ask. I ask myself the same thing.

"Hi, my name is Belinda. I'm Jack's wife and you're not," she says. I'm thinking, very unusual introduction. The crowd laughs appreciatively, like how cute is that. She wears a black leather jacket over a scuffed-up white T-shirt, as if she's been under the car or messing with the bike, and a red skirt that is too small in just the way you might hope for it to be too small. She is entirely alluring in a completely puzzling way.

"I won't keep you," she says. I want her to keep me.

"Here he is now," she says, and extends her arm out in the direction of a man who is anything but handsome. He is untidy and old, late sixties maybe. From the waist down—rock and roll has-been, black jeans, yellow Converse sneakers. From the waist up—contractor whose bid you'd never trust, plaid work shirt, poor-fitting denim jacket, pockets bulging with note paper.

"Good evening," he says in the relaxed style of a welcomed monarch. Really have trouble with relaxed people. Belinda slinks off, which I'm not happy about. I strain my neck to see where she went, but I can't find her.

"I hope you will bear with me while I read a handful of poems," Jack says. I hate the not very credible modesty that accompanies the massively accomplished. Although in my head I'm preparing myself to sound courteous and underwhelmed should I ever come face to face with an adoring crowd. They bear with him all right. An almost reverent silence falls over the place. I feel a cough coming on, but I suppress it. I don't want to be the noise-making heretic drawing attention away from literature incarnate. Jack reads his handful. One describes the crumbling facade of a building slated for demolition. The building has something to do with the ankles of a raven-haired newlywed already unsure about her marriage. It's poetry, so you can connect any ass thing together you want. I'm not complaining. Actually, I'm taken with it, falling under the spell or whatever. In another of his poems, a man in the upstairs bedroom of his house studies a nude photo of a girlfriend who has stopped calling while homeless youths break his car windows and steal the vehicle. I can relate to that, but I'm not sure why. I rely on public transport and no one I know has left me with a nude photo.

A few of the women in the audience looked moved or disturbed; I can't tell which. One is teary. I want to be able to write poems that make women teary. That would be cool, and that would be "important" or something. My trouble is I always want to do what someone else is able to do. Jack is done with the poems and the Q and A is starting up. My hand goes up automatically; it's like it's doing it without my consent. Jack goes right for me, looking me dead in the eye, and I feel shaky.

"What's your question?" he says, on account of me not having said anything.

"Oh," I say. I feel desperate and afraid that no more words are coming. "Well, I was wondering if there are particular times of the day that work best for you."

"To what?" he says. I swear I hear faint laughter coming from the crowd.

"Oh, fuck," I say. Yes, I actually say oh, fuck. "To write, of course, sorry." You can imagine how I'm feeling because yeah, public humiliation has never been among my favorite things.

"I like your question," he says. He says it so personally, so sincerely, like he's been waiting a lifetime for me to show up and ask one of the most over-asked, brain-dead questions writers get asked all the time. That faint laughter is history now. A respectful silence has returned.

"It's night-time for me, too late at night to tell you the truth, interferes with my sleep, aggravates my wife, makes me grumpy the next morning, but it's the only time I can manage it," he says. He's speaking to me with such regard. I'm getting warm. I watch his lips. I adjust myself in my seat. Suddenly, posture seems important. I want my posture to say, thank you, you're a genius, you pulled me from the fire, I freaking love you. I raise my shoulders and straighten my spine; no more slumping for me.

When he's done reading, I head like a man on a mission over to the counter to buy his book of poems. I hold that book of poems close to my chest, thinking irrationally that it may be taken from me by a truly informed literary type who is sure I won't know how to make proper use of it.

# ADMIRATION

## I.

**JOE WANTS TO WRITE**, or rather he wants to do something and he's not going to take up whitewater rafting. Joe doesn't worry about money, having had a grandmother who found reasons to like him. He worries about everything else, fears an early death, believes he hasn't lived much anyway, even now, before his early death. Thinks about women a lot, maybe all the time. Depending on how one defines "all the time." For instance, he could be doing something pedestrian like removing the wrapping from a hamburger at McDonald's, and though he knows there will be no woman under the wrapping, that this is just a straightforward desire for a cheap lunch, still he imagines a woman there eating one with him. Or he imagines never again eating a hamburger from McDonald's because a devotedly vegetarian woman has brought her long legs into his likely-to-be-short life.

Joe looks up to a local writer whose name is Walter. Walter has the air and confidence of a highly regarded, prizewinning type of writer, although he is neither. Joe finds this quality as admirable as it is mysterious and offers Walter help with paperwork and household chores in exchange for writing lessons. The lessons are unusual. Walter looks over Joe's work every two weeks and asks Joe not to write a lot, since he gets tired reading his stuff. At first Joe finds this insulting, but Walter says a few charming things that Joe can no longer recall, which convince him it's actually flattering. Walter's instruction to Joe is to pay attention to what's around him and curb as few impulses as possible, which is hard since pretty much all Joe has ever done is curb impulses. Then there's Walter's wife, Beatrice, with whom Joe would love to not curb an impulse. Not an option because Walter would kill him. And once dead, the opportunity for engagement in extra-marital affairs is greatly diminished. Unless he has that all wrong, and clandestine behavior is all the rage in the post-life dimension, and this is why we don't see the dead on account of how damn sneaky they are. But he does glance at Beatrice covertly. Once, she caught him doing it; he blushed profusely, moving his head rapidly in every direction, as if to imply he'd been scanning the room in an impartial frenzy when his eyes accidentally landed on her. Beatrice is in her mid-forties and not an obvious beauty. Her nose looks like it's been in bar fights, her lips are mammoth, her breasts are full and relaxed, free of the rigidity of ones that have been tampered with. Untampered-with breasts are, well, more breast-like in Joe's opinion. He doesn't know who he might share this opinion with, since it seems inherently awkward. For instance, when he imagines a woman, say a woman eerily similar in appearance to Beatrice, and if this imagined woman were to remove her bra, he can't picture himself saying like, "Phew, I really like your unaltered breasts." That would be sexually Aspergersy and tactless even though that's what he'd be feeling. This to Joe is one of the challenges when it comes to the now popular idea of the authentic life.

## II.

The three of them are out together, a frequent occurrence. Why Joe has become part of the social circumstance of their marriage he does not know, despite the pleasure he takes in it.

Walter likes to drink and talk, and Joe is a good listener. Walter tells Joe his work is coming along; he's even beginning to enjoy some of his sentences. With time and courage, Walter says, he could become a fine writer. It's at moments like these that Joe feels that he has a reason to live, the challenge for Joe being the large swaths of time in between moments like these. Beatrice says that Joe might benefit from a real job while his metamorphosis into writer is taking place. That hurts. He does not know if Walter shows Beatrice his writing and has been afraid to ask, fearing her commentary might be withering, and a bad review from someone you can't take your eyes off is a bridge straight to hell, the way Joe sees bridges.

"You need to take risks, talk to strangers. Your own life's material is limiting, and Beatrice and I don't want you writing about us, do we sweetie?"

"I wouldn't mind if the writing is good," she says. A flash of wild hope runs through Joe just as he is settling into a regular bout of self-loathing.

Walter is distracted; an aging cocktail waitress is at their table, her beauty clock still ticking. The waitress wants to know if they have everything they need.

"Needs are numberless, unfathomable," Walter says. Joe wishes he could speak this way to people. The waitress smiles. Her crooked yellow teeth are not so unappetizing as to detract from a still shapely mouth. Beatrice's mouth tightens, she moves around on her chair as if it has suddenly become too small or her bottom has gotten larger or something.

"Vodka on the rocks," Walter says.

"Sure hon," the waitress says, bending forward, her liberally exposed cleavage hanging over their table like a lewd mascot. She asks Beatrice the same question.

"White wine, please," Beatrice says.

"I'll have the same," Walter says, wanting to show solidarity.

The waitress leaves to get the drinks. As she walks away, Walter takes in every inch. Joe feels bad for Beatrice, but she shows no sign of irritation. In fact, she watches too, as if along with her husband she is fascinated with the woman's gait.

With the waitress gone, Walter addresses Joe again.

"Pick a person who's of interest to you, ask them about their life. Everyone suffers from the delusion that their life is interesting."

Beatrice is of interest to him, but he can't pick her.

Walter gets up to use the john.

A shocking thing happens. Joe feels a kick from under the table. It can only be Beatrice kicking him; no one else is there. She has never made physical contact with him, not even a handshake. He has the strangest sensation, feeling like his body has been returned to him, as if for the longest time it had been in someone else's possession. He looks at her expecting her to say something, confirm

11

that there was a kick and that she delivered it. She looks back, not saying a word. Just as Joe is questioning whether it happened at all, a second kick arrives, quite firm. There might be bruising, Joe thinks, and then he chastises himself for having such a trivial thought in a moment of great and majestic intrigue.

"You could interview me," Beatrice says.

"I could?" Joe says.

"It would have to be private, just between the two of us. A room without too much light. I imagine you'd want me in lingerie, for interview purposes of course. Would add a compelling tension, don't you think?"

Joe wonders if tension is important in interviews, but then he realizes this is about something else and that she must really be upset about the waitress.

"Beatrice," he says, but cannot come up with more.

"I'm serious," she says.

Joe sees Walter emerge from the bathroom.

He has never been sadder to see a male figure exit a public toilet.

Beatrice kicks him again and winks. Although enjoying it, Joe hopes it will end when Walter sits back down.

Walter sits back down.

Beatrice says, "I think the waitress is a slut."

It gets very quiet at the table. Joe hopes he doesn't have to weigh in on whether the waitress is a slut or not because, if anything is a sure bet to introduce compelling tension, that would be it.

"Yes, she probably is," Walter says as if he's agreeing that, given the chilly weather, a winter coat is in order.

Joe is relieved.

Walter takes Beatrice's hand and looks into her eyes. Unlike the sharp, lusty look of a pickpocket he'd given the waitress, his gaze is deep and full of affection. Joe feels jealous. He chides himself for such foolishness. A woman kicking you under the table does not mean she has fallen out of love with her husband.

Nevertheless, he is very, very jealous, and he comforts himself with the thought that Walter is at an age likely to be coincident with an enlarged prostate, so he has good reason to hope for more bathroom breaks.

And hope he does.

# UNWISE

**IT WASN'T THAT I** got the idea to have an affair with my mentor's wife. I didn't have the idea, I had the fantasy, which is a different thing, practically harmless. She's the one who had the idea. Was it because she could tell I was having the fantasy and she wanted to show me what reality looked like?

It started in a supermarket, not a setting I'd ever have associated with the beginning of torrid relations, but then again, I'd had no torrid relations. We were on a grocery run for her husband. Vegetables were needed to go with their steak and he was out of whiskey. We were very quiet and I was wishing I had the gift of gab, being seldom alone with her, and I wanted to be able to say a clever thing or two, make her smile. We'd just bagged some Brussels sprouts when she grabbed my arm so hard it hurt. She looked at me very directly. I wanted her to loosen her grip, but at the same time I was glad she had hold of me.

"Matt, I need a distraction in my life right now. I want us to sleep together, like next week. I don't enjoy simply thinking about it, I hope to like doing it." I don't like to admit this, but her tone was not brimming with optimism.

"And I don't want you taking this the wrong way," she added. I was without a way of any kind to take it.

Her demeanor was not in the least bit lighthearted.

Her face got closer to mine.

"I'm creatively blocked—my husband is promiscuous, and you're always around."

I could feel her breath on my face, the intense proximity of her body. I was under a kind of erotic duress.

"Oh," I said. Longer sentences felt out of reach.

"You're malleable, and I need a man who'll take directions," she said. I would take directions, that was true. If I was going to be sleeping with my mentor's wife, I would be sincerely grateful for directions.

"I have a hunch you can provide relief, perhaps even inspiration," she said. I had no idea what she meant or what had led her to such a conclusion. I was wonderstruck. No woman would ever speak this way to me again, of that I was certain.

"I want us to work on a schedule. An organized approach is best, don't you think?" she said.

I felt sure there was no orderly path to spending time in bed with my mentor's wife. Doug, her husband, was a man I admired, a man who'd thrown me a lifeline when I was down in the dumps. I was counting on him to usher me into a creative, worthwhile life. He was a poet, and I aspired to be something of that sort. You don't sleep with that man's wife, but then again, you don't expect her to suggest it.

"I'm thinking once a week for about an hour and a half, depending on your skills," she said, smiling.

I did not think that it was even an option because of what it would do to my relationship with Doug. If I lost Doug, what would I have been left with? She had not implied that she was looking to replace her husband. An hour and a half a week was a finite period of time, and by the sounds of it she was seeking the intimate encounter to help with a clogged creative pipe. She was a short-story writer. Perhaps she needed to engage in bizarre and doomed activity so she could pen edgier fiction. I stood there looking at her, sure I was about to say that, although this was the most flattering proposal I'd ever received or ever expected to receive, there was no way I could go along with it. I readied myself for the strong statement that never came.

"I don't want you pretending to be gallant, principled, and loyal. That would be tiresome. Most men would jump at the chance to sleep with me."

I was struck by her clairvoyance. Loyalty and principle were key parts of the presentation I would have made, given a little more time.

"I'm thinking about the Seascape Motel, the one with the big blue sign you see from the freeway. Do you know it?"

"I've seen it."

"Tuesday at three works for me. Doug isn't home till five-thirty. He's very serious about his poetry students on that particular day, probably because he's fucking one of them."

"Sarah, this is not something I can do, you must know that."

"I want you to listen to me closely because we don't have a lot of time. We are not going to get into a lot of talk about this. A woman—a wife—doesn't make a decision like this lightly. I want you to know I'm deadly serious. I've made up my mind. It's important for you to know, since you're involved."

I told myself I was not involved, not yet.

"I can't," I said.

"Give me a break, for fuck's sake. Can we be real here for a moment? How often do you expect to get an offer like this?"

"Never again, I imagine. And of course I would love to, but your husband means a lot to me; he has changed my life."

"I like him too, Matt, but that's neither here nor there. In any case, he stands to benefit from an improvement in my mood. You'll be doing him a favor—think of it that way."

I did not believe that was a credible way to look at it.

"I can't, Sarah. It stands to destroy a relationship I cherish."

"Matt, try not to be such a drama queen. I'll give you something to cherish, believe me."

She winked at me. I felt I'd been let into a club I was in no way credentialed for. The grip I had on my protests came loose.

And something about that wink, what I imagined it promised, broke the dam.

"I believe you," I said. A woman I'd found mesmerizingly attractive was putting her foot down, forbidding me to wiggle out of sleeping with her.

It was hard to think of this as bad news.

"So it's a date then?" she said.

"It is," I replied.

Back in my apartment that evening I was jumpy as hell. I knew I'd agreed to something crazy. In a small, suicidal type of way, I was glad I had.

But Doug had welcomed me into his life, told me my writing had potential. I had felt like a full-fledged person in his company.

Now I'd made a plan to sleep with his wife.

I made several trips to the bathroom, certain I was about to vomit.

The morning of our *date* I drank a glass of vodka but remained terribly uneasy, the way you can be when you've had one of those lifelike dreams in which you've knocked someone off, or someone is close to knocking you off, and the police know that either you're the killer or you're about to be killed. But it doesn't matter which because they just can't get there in time to prevent it.

# TAKE TWO

## I. [THE TIME HAS COME]

**IT DOES TAKE MORE** than one. You've tried it on
your own. Not working. Move away from your private
adventure in front of the laptop's glowing screen. Look
up from your soiled lap. Return the toilet roll to the
bathroom. A small quiet mess is not a life. Take a chance.
Ask Janet out. She is in this world for a short time, like
you. See, you do have something in common. People
underestimate the similarity they share on account of
what waits for them at the end, which is not by the way, a
suggestion to bring it up. Talk of mortality as an opening
gambit is pretty much a buzzkill.

## 2. [IMPEDIMENTS]

I agree. When Janet passes your office desk, she does
exude what could be interpreted as a mild case of
contempt. It does seem subtly directed at you. I want to
emphasize the word subtle here. It is not extreme. It is
not hate. Listen, Janet is the only uncoupled woman you
know, and whatever way you've been broadcasting your
appeal on romance-promising websites, it's not working.
You were shooting for originality, didn't want to go the
"walks on the beach," "trip to the wine country" route,
but posting a prose poem on the unexpected romance
that blossoms from a car-jacking may have been taking
the "original" approach in a worrisome direction, from
the point of view of potential respondents. There were
one or two, but I can tell you for a fact that the woman
you were scheduled to meet last Tuesday at Philz Coffee,

the blonde whose dating website name was Sandra, was the very same woman who, when you went up and asked her if she was Sandra, lied, telling you her name was Candace and that she was waiting for her husband. She was not waiting for her husband. She has no husband. Up until you walked in, it was you she was waiting for. Don't spend a lot of time thinking about this. Let's say initial impressions are not your strong suit. It doesn't matter. Initial impressions are mostly fraudulent, which brings me back to Janet. She at least knows you. Over the years, she's laughed at one, maybe two of your jokes. Value those memories. Read things into them.

## 3. [DOUBTS AND POSSIBILITIES]

Janet's not involved with anyone, hasn't been for years. Her volatility, her high-decibel rages may keep men at bay. I know you've been on the receiving end of those, but you WERE missing deadlines, and she is on the Company Leadership Team. She has a job to do. Ask her out. Both your clocks are ticking. She might want kids. After a while you can talk her into an anger management class, especially if she wants kids. You don't want her going ballistic on the toddlers. Perhaps she's great in bed, whatever that means. You've heard it said. It's brought up everywhere, but you've never had the nerve to ask someone for a definition. What you know so far is this: if a woman takes off her clothes and gets in bed with you, that pretty much comes down to great. The "great in bed" sentence bandied about so casually by so many who, frighteningly, may in fact know what it means, makes you anxious since no former girlfriend has ever described you that way. Life's a risk. Another person is a nerve-wracking proposition. So what? Just ask. At a minimum you'll surprise her. She could use a surprise.

## 4. [AND THEN...]

You are by the water cooler with her. You planned it.
Good work. She got back early from lunch. You didn't
go to lunch, you just waited. You kept getting up from
your desk, peeking into the hallway, praying she'd be back
first, praying she was one of an ever-increasing number
of people focused on hydrating themselves at regular
intervals. You've skipped a lot of lunches waiting for this
to work out. And she's back way early, fifteen minutes or
more. The office is quiet as church.

"What are you doing here?" she says.

You never noticed before, but she has a small gap between
her front teeth. How could you have missed that? It's
terribly appealing. An opening where you didn't expect to
find one.

"You're not going to believe it, but I want to ask you
out," you say, taking pride in your moment of valor no
matter how tentative it might sound. Janet looks at you
as if she were studying a very unusual plant, one she has
never seen and does not know the name of but that has
somehow suddenly popped up in her garden. The fact
that time is passing by and she has not said the word no,
or started screaming at you about the utter disregard for
the standards of the workplace you are demonstrating by
your dreamy, trance-like staring at her front teeth and
your bizarre request to date her—this very fact, along with
the stunned silence the two of you share, has your body
begin to respond as if in fact she will say yes, as if at some

21

inevitable time in the future this fearsome and attractive member of the Company Leadership Team will be treating you to undreamed-of sights and experiences.

## 5. [HOME FREE?]

The two of you are at her place. You think the risk of failure (which is the risk of life, isn't it, every minute?) is lower. You have made it from the water cooler to her actual home. You are through the door. It's true she did have a cocktail at dinner, but she appears in charge of her wits. You must be likeable. You must be of interest. Surely you are not through the door solely on the strength of one quickly consumed alcoholic beverage. Janet is on the Company Leadership Team. She is a substantive person. Mild inebriation would neither diminish her character nor reduce her standards, although it may lower her expectations, which would not be so bad. Not long after you enter her habitat, she sits comfortably down on her beige Italian leather sofa in her spare but tastefully appointed living room, kicks off her shoes, and curls up her legs. Because you are in her house, because she has let you in, you are, let's say, newly entitled to take a seat beside her. On account of such mounting evidence, there is an understanding that there will be a kiss. Something has to come next.

## 6. [FLASHBACK]

You remember the beginning of this kissing business, how you stumbled into it at fourteen. You'd lived a sheltered life and certainly hadn't imagined it to be the way it turned out: a welcomed entrance into the watery dark cave of another person's complete and total mouth, an exploration of mystery and delight possessing an ecstatic quality, one more astonishing than a triple scoop of ice cream with an open bar of choice toppings. At that tender age, it was inconceivable that a girl who had initiated you thusly, and provided safe passage into her extraordinary cavity, from where at other times her sardonic teenage sentences were launched with aplomb—that that same girl who had ushered you into a realm and onto a ride more exhilarating and transcendent that any dreamed up by Disneyland, would be bestowing much the same rapturous treatment on an entirely different boy a mere two weeks later. Adult pain made its first showing. It hurt like hell. You told your mother. She showed no sympathy.

## 7. [THE PRESENT]

And now, just shy of middle age, you discover again a magic you assumed had long since expired, killed off by the adult reality of too many choices. Specifically, the choices all four of your ex-girlfriends made after sampling you because tonight your tongue, the tongue that is uniquely yours, the one that came with your body, has been given the right and privilege to pay a visit to that heart-stopping little gap between Janet's two front teeth. Take a bow, fella.

You begin again. Every feeling of defeat, every oddly-written and possibly ill-advised dating website personal profile, every petty humiliation suffered at the hands of desire, every lonely and basically unimaginative sexual fantasy you've subjected yourself to will vanish into forgotten dust.

Here's what you will call it.

You will call it the past.

# DATE

**YOU TAKE A RISK**. What is there left to take, if not a risk?
She asked you out. Amazing of her to do that this late
in the game when you are several emotionally drought-
ridden scenes into what has to be Act Four of your life.

Let's put it this way, that within the room you have for
improvements are a whole lot of improvements that have
not been made and a sufficient number of decades have
gone by for you to be under the ever-more-convincing
impression that they will never be. In other words, you get
to die before you have sorted out how to live.

But she asked.

She doesn't even know you, which is probably what
sparked her interest. She delivered some apparently
important papers to your office so it was a chance
encounter. Who cares if Larry told you that every chance
encounter is an act of desperation disguised as a chance
encounter?

Larry has become sour living with just the one cat and two
reptiles.

Some advice: Bring your listening ears. Men often leave
them in the car. Be attentive, ask questions, but don't
grill her. She's not under arrest. Cut through the jungle of
awkwardness and speak of your life. Conveniently, a life
with its ups and downs, triumphs and disappointments
etc, provides the content for conversation. Conversation
requires content. It's not enough to simply have answered

in the affirmative once the miracle of her date request burst through the gloom of your native weather. You will need to say stuff, discover areas of commonality or invent them. A really good date can feel like two total strangers back from a separate but equally desolate wilderness clutching a note that appears to have the same stuff written on it. That is, if you are both willing to stretch interpretation into very elastic places.

With luck, the pair of you may yet get to marvel at all the congruity that can make itself known in the course of one mere evening.

Be sure to leave out any reference to prior desolation, chronic self-doubt, and that sizable lake of despair you've been splashing around in—for happiness has no past. It begins as the two of you step out into the night.

It can't be a Beckett play, a lonely waiting both of you do for the arrival of meaning.

Godot isn't coming. Seriously, you don't even want him around, such a killjoy.

It needs to be more like a musical. Picture Marilyn Monroe's dress blowing up over a ventilation grate. Put a metaphorical umbrella in your hand, dance in the rain. But don't sing. What did your last girlfriend say? "Honey, you're totally tone deaf." Not encouraging. But at least she said honey. Cleave to the happy part of that sentence.

Next:

You are at her place. Toward the end of dinner, she just

came right out and invited you, said something like, "Want to come over?" Over where, you asked yourself, her side of the table? No, she couldn't mean that. She must mean the other thing, the vast thing. You had not finished dessert. You didn't care if you ever ate again. The bill unpaid, you reached for your wallet. She waited on an answer. Her eyes were beautiful. Whatever she had meant, you were in the yes column, mesmerized as you were by her fire-engine-red lips, which you'd seen open and close like the trailer for the best movie that will ever come out. You felt intensely grateful for the invention of lipstick, a clear triumph of science. Wanted to ask everyone in the restaurant, "Do you see those lips? Can you believe that color?" And it was only going to get more insanely pleasurable. Someone upstairs was leveling the playing field. "My place," she said. Could there be two more intoxicating words in the English language? Somehow you had met her standards, or she'd abandoned standards, decided to try something else, standards not having done the trick. When you are in her bathroom peeing, and the strong stream of your newly reinvigorated urine confidently hits the side of her toilet bowl, it will feel like Heaven's waiting room.

You will fill up with an immensity of feeling natural to those who have crossed from the dreariness of everyday life into an exalted dimension. The formerly locked door to this exclusive club has flown open. Think of the others out there. Compare them to your new self. Consider if a stranger came now to her door and knocked to ask, "Miss, do you mind if I use your toilet?" She would answer, "Certainly not, unwanted stranger." And what did she say to you? "Come on in!" You will look at yourself in her bathroom mirror. That's not vanity. Everyone in that room would look. You will take a moment to wink at the man who has been invited to become her lover. That's you, remember. And when the time comes for you to emerge from that small kingdom of shower curtain, sink, and bowl, it will not be simply pleasure you anticipate but salvation. You have cut your ties with reality. What had it ever done for you anyway?

You'll picture her out there delicately freeing a lacy undergarment that lived until now in a perfumed box from Paris, sequestered away in her secret treasure trove of erotic splendor.

For just this moment.

She is gorgeous. The way those ears are placed on her head, her freckled legs, her full lips. Who thinks up stuff like that?

You talk about writers. She has strong opinions. Amazingly, you find yourself agreeing with all of them. She starts to make tea. You say, "I can do that." You want to show her that you are the type of man who can take the tea-making reins at a moment's notice. She lets you, which you interpret as yielding. Yielding seems like a wonderful omen. It's going so well.

Next:

The morning light streams in her window. It's so bright you're tempted to put sunglasses on, but then she'd be waking up to a man wearing sunglasses, which would be odd. Things had turned odd enough, no need for you to add an absurd postscript to a recently collapsed empire.

She wakes up and looks at you like you were once a brightly colored fish that she found grey and dead the next morning, floating in its bowl. But you are alive and breathing on land. You are no fish nor have you ever been. Something went awry. Was it the tentative way you reached for her shoulders? Should your approach have had more surefootedness, steelier determination? Why did she say so quickly, as you reached here and there trying to find a landing spot that pleased her, "Let's go to sleep now and talk about it in the morning?"

"We tried our best," she says, like there was another team, a secret team, one you didn't see that wound up handing you defeat. And wouldn't you like to be a fly on the wall of that invisible locker room? But you're not. You are neither fish nor fly. She is naked. That much did happen. You look at her with the same face that gazed triumphantly into her bathroom mirror only a few hours ago. Her small, miraculous breasts are now mere inches from your face. It's as though you've been ushered through the portal to Paradise just to see what it looks like for a minute. She reaches for her shirt. You wish she wouldn't. Her underarms are unshaven, a smattering of light colored hairs. It is a mystery to you what women hold on to and what they dispense with.

She gives you a peck on the cheek.

The dreaded peck: that homeopathic distillation of a kiss; the consolation prize that never consoles; the certain seal of ending.

# MIXED FORMULA

**YOU HAVE NO FAITH** in the words of others. Even your own thoughts are an endless stream of fraudulent ticker tape. Occasionally a person speaks and you listen. Usually it's a woman. A morsel from such a source can still sound digestible, but you might be making that up for spurious reasons or for the hope of comfort you imagine might come from burying your hypothetical head into her hypothetical bosom, whoever she might be, with her half overheard sentences trailing off into the darker corners of a bar for the terminally sad. That was the last time your ears pricked up, wasn't it? Where did it happen? You've already forgotten. You've embraced the jaundiced view. You started out hopeful enough but never encountered depth that didn't make you want to drain the pool. What made you always yank the chain that held the plug? Why were you suspicious of content and the verbal elaborations people used to point to something called themselves? You were an early opponent of too much information, we'll give you that. You were in the vanguard of withdrawal. Now you sit in a soiled bathrobe with the hood pulled up like a defrocked monastic deposited in a downtown Oakland condo, the view sealed off with tragic curtains. You're a dour creature. And then it happens. The dormant machinery of your life cranks up. Light is present, and it's glaring. You can't access your bearings and you're glad, although glad doesn't quite capture it. You're captured. She comes out of nowhere, the one place you forgot to look. She makes a sizable offer. The sheer scale of it makes it non-optional, or so you think. Actually, you've stopped thinking. A silenced mind, the goal of mystics, the trademark of happiness. It is yours in the split second that follows her saying:

"Undress me."

You don't know her. Because once you know a person, once their material is spilling into your life like four rooms of unpacked boxes, do they ever say undress me in that tone of voice? And then, quite unexpectedly, you have a sense of déjà vu, and you realize maybe you do know her, kind of. Wasn't it your friend Alec who introduced you to her back in the day? Wasn't that the woman with the clammy handshake, the triumphant cleavage, the long legs? Weren't they married? They probably were. Alec probably introduced you. He probably said, "This is my wife, Sylvia." He probably had a proud look. Alec had too many proud looks for his own good. Perhaps they tired her out.

Right now, she's wide awake.

"What are you waiting for?" Sylvia says.

Do you even know where you are? Whose room is this? How did you get here? You think she drove? That's certainly possible; she's got the wheel, that's for sure. Did you tie up loose ends before coming? Isn't that what dragged you down in the first place, loose ends, the firing squad of ongoing tasks, attributes of real adult life? Which reminds me: where's your mother? Did you forget about her, your only surviving parent? Did she escape your notice? Convenient, putting your mother aside while you do what exactly?

"Start with my blouse," Sylvia says.

It's a vintage blouse, light blue, prim, almost Victorian. Her manner seems at odds with her appearance as if she's crossed from a drawing room in a Jane Austen novel into a 1970s soft-core movie. Are you going to lift your trembling hands to those buttons? Why do the words *hope chest* keep springing to mind? Can you find a graceful path to Sylvia's breasts, and not lunge like a starving man for a scrap of food? This is a challenge you are up for, I'm guessing, something to get you out of the house. Your mother managed the house, raised you kids, worked damn hard, too. Someone had to pick up the slack given your father's, shall we say, lackluster work ethic. Did you leave your elderly mother at the bus stop, the wrong bus stop maybe? Was that deliberate, a design to facilitate your desires, now that they seem to be back? What if she's irretrievable, that mother of yours? What if she never gets home? Won't you ask yourself how you could have misplaced her so convincingly?

Sylvia's blouse is off. You may be responsible for that, unless she grew tired of waiting and did it herself.

"My bra, can you help with that?" she asks, which might be a clue. What does this clue reveal about your commitment, your initiative, your sense of responsibility, about what may have happened between you and Sylvia, about the possible location of your mother, if she is still with us, if she has not yet gone from this world? Was your mother once in a room like this, a dark room, a room off the beaten track, taking a break from being beaten down? Was there another man, one different from your lethargic pop with his petty tyrannies? In a musty room like this? Your mom, the competent hands of a stranger on her, the dexterous hands of a hard working man, who could manage, who could lead, lead your mother to a place like this, remove her garments, and her smiling, an expression of delight filling her usually melancholy face? A man who knows what he's doing at last. Might those have been your mother's thoughts? You are in strange terrain and bras can be a tricky operation, isn't that so? Hooks and what have you. You see Sylvia's breasts. They have made their way out into the open, free of confinement, a wild and blooming garden. You had filed her away under: wife of Alec, wet handshake. And now that same woman brings you to life. Did you help? Have you ever helped anyone? In the end, did you do your fair share? Is that how Sylvia's breasts came out, as a result of your good effort?

Will there be a funeral for your mother if the worst comes to pass? Of course there will be a funeral, if they can find her to bury her, that is. She will have to be tracked down first. Even a dead person must be discovered and returned in order to be laid to rest. You know that.

"You can touch me," Sylvia says.

# WHO?

**I WENT SOMEPLACE AND** heard a person mention me, mention me by name. I got very excited, more excited than I'd been in years, because this person, whoever they were, was not my uncle, sister, or coworker. I was so looking forward to making this person's acquaintance and getting the entire backstory in regard to how they became aware of me and, perhaps more importantly, discovering the component factors that led them to speak of me to others. I'd always dreamed of being spoken of to others by someone other than myself. Naturally I was curious in regard to what my name, and therefore my person, meant to the speaker of it. And I was almost desperate to find out how many other times they had spoken of me, and to how many people exactly. It was probably too much to hope for an exact count, but I would settle for an approximate number. Were there particular settings and contexts that prompted them to mention me more than at other times? And if indeed there were, might more of such contexts be encouraged? That would certainly be my wish. I knew enough to be subtle in suggesting it. It would be too much, for instance, to imagine people bringing my name up before making love, but I just couldn't help but imagine it, and so I did. I started to hope that this possible utterance of my name, when utilized right before lovemaking, might suffuse the atmosphere with extra promise, the bedroom being on certain occasions, a bit of a roll of the dice. It would comfort me to hear (through the grapevine, of course) that when my name was, shall we say, whispered into the ear of one of the lovers, momentum did not falter or fade, the impersonation of fulfillment was not called on to make an appearance, and the train actually arrived at the station. This was a most satisfying contemplation, since its thoughtful origins would make my joy at having heard my name mentioned larger than the pleasure that accompanies recognition, since I'd now begun to picture how others might also benefit from it. When celebrating one's self, it is prudent to balance out one's heady feeling with some consideration for people in general. I was suddenly aware of a wise and expansive aspect of my character that must have lain dormant until this moment. Well, it was time to introduce myself to the person who had spoken of me, but it was a crowded room and when I looked around I no longer saw the person from whose mouth my name had sprung. I became more distressed than I'd been in years and was visited there and then by an unimaginable sensation of loss. After all, it had only been a moment ago that I had, for the first time in life, felt myself publicly found. When I finally emerged from a deep and familiar sense of invisibility, I asked myself, "Is there a way forward?" No clear answer presented itself, so I went up to the first person I saw—although in truth I saw a lot of people, but I picked one out of the many in the same way that I had been picked out to be spoken of to the many ever so recently—and I asked this selected person— desperate as I was for a way forward—I asked him, "Have you seen the person who spoke of me?"

"And who might you be?" he replied.

This was a question I'd always feared might come. I was not prepared for it because I had not, despite years of looking into the matter, been able to come to a firm or even wobbly conclusion on the subject. There I was, the prisoner of a brutal irony at the very moment when my name had been mentioned. I would have had the opportunity to inquire as to why it had been, and what exactly it signified, and thus got to know more, or at least got to know something about myself from an outside and hopefully objective source, when at that very moment the messenger vanished into thin air.

"How do you mean?" I asked, hoping for an escape hatch by replying to his penetrating question with a question of my own.

"Well, how can I tell you if I've heard you brought up if I don't know who you are?"

"Raymond," I said, "I'm Raymond."

It wasn't true. I didn't even look like a Raymond. If anyone actually knew me, they'd know my name was Paul.

"Never heard of you," he said, and walked away.

# POETRY

**MY WIFE AT HER** laptop looking at that Poem of The Day business. A picture of the poet sits comfortably beside the poem. "She's sexy," I say, thinking that later I'd like to get to the bottom of perceptions like these.

"I knew you'd think that," my wife says. "She's one of those petite types you go for, nothing like me."

I'm taken by the poet's blonde bobbed hair blowing slightly in the desert wind. My wife says she lives in Joshua Tree as if she's about to give me her address and has the address of all petite, wind-blown poets posing for pictures in silent, rock-strewn landscapes. I tell my wife my eyes are not so good and that I don't detect anything particularly petite about her.

"You should go off with them," my wife says.

"Them?" I say.

"The desert poets," she says. I begin picturing the poets, each in their own adobe hut, each at their writing desk, each just a cactus or two down from their neighbor. They become dear to me and I realize I must make the journey, being, after all, a pilgrim in the way of words. I'll knock on each door with the simple message, "My wife sent me." An authentic statement is naturally endearing, so I'm certain to be ushered in. One wants to be ushered in after a long trek through blazing heat; one craves the comfort offered by a stanza or two; one seeks the stimulation a rollicking sestina brings. "How I appreciate your writing implement," I'll say, speaking directly from the heart. Why I'd never thought of making such a tour before is beyond me. You can live decade after decade oblivious to your true calling. I start to pack and my wife asks me where the fuck I think I'm going. "To visit the desert poets," I say. I don't think she cares for my answer, which is probably what has her threaten to kill me. I take my wife seriously, so I put off my trip for the time being.

The Poem of the Day no longer prints a picture of the poet off to the side. If you scroll down, a habit that requires either an innate optimism or Puritan work ethic, you will see the picture of the poet. But by the time I get that far, despair has set in and I've lost all longing for human contact.

# UNGLUED

**IT MIGHT HAVE BEEN** the coffee. I was exuberant, untethered. Anything seemed possible. The throbbing of desire, a result perhaps of ye old unlived life, coursed through me. I wrote to Bob, telling him a simple truth: the sight of his wife's ankles caused me to swoon. Not to the point of passing out, but almost. I thought he'd be glad to hear an honest, unfiltered confession; that it would draw us closer. Who knows how many men before me had teetered on the brink after just such a vision, and kept it to themselves? Cowards. I would be the one to speak up. And I meant the whole thing as a compliment to him. He had chosen her. Well done, I wanted to say. Bravo.

In the letter, I neglected to mention his ankles, which I thought might be why I did not hear anything back. When I think of his ankles, which isn't often, I imagine them covered up by those white socks that come in packets of three from garishly lit sporting goods stores. Those are terrible socks. I wear them myself so I speak from experience. Those damn socks, in their sporty little packets, are filled with irony. Their design hints at athleticism. Their true nature, once unmasked, is entirely devoid of athleticism. Your poor feet can barely breathe in those things. Believe me in those socks there is no three-minute mile in your future. I feel sorry for Bob when I think of his poor ankles trapped in such suffocating encasements while his wife goes about boldly displaying hers. The scales of justice so improperly tilted.

I wish he'd write me back.

I thought to send a follow-up letter. I couldn't stop thinking about it. Everywhere I went I was silently composing it. What I would say, how I might say it, became the central meaning of my life, which I was grateful for since I had been on the lookout for a central meaning. I thought it inadvisable to begin the letter with an outright apology for making so much of his wife's ankles because that would remind him of what had become a painful subject if, in fact, that is what it had become. On the other hand, if I left out the matter entirely and simply shot the breeze, would he take that as an insult to his intelligence or even conclude that I had reassessed my perspective on his wife's ankles, demoting them on the scale of desirables down to humdrum, run-of-the-mill body parts, dully related to the human skeleton, things that would still hang around after the rest of her was gone? That would be quite a downgrade, and anyway one should not remind a man of the perishable nature of his wife. I decided the best strategy was to act as if no breach had occurred and that there was no significance to the deathly silence that had fallen between us. And that, regardless of what he may have thought, there had been no letter. The letter I was busy composing would count as my first correspondence. Any letter he may have received earlier had come from someone claiming to be me, dispatching inappropriate sentiments through the U.S. Mail.

Bizarre forgeries sent by an obviously deranged individual.

My new letter would take the form of an invitation, feeling as I did that only more time in each other's company could provide the balm needed to heal the wounds caused by the author of the first letter. Let's refer to him as the imposter. This invitation would serve as a testing ground into which I would bravely enter to right what might have been a wrong, readying myself to do battle with temptation no matter how formidable. It required inventive planning. Everything was survivable if all I was faced with was a from-the-waist-up version of Bob's wife. True, all parts of her were charming. Trinkets of loveliness abounded on her person, little treasure chests opened like drawers in unusual places, sparkling and silently communicative. The way her breath seemed to snake through her upper body put me in mind of a gothic novel I could not recall the title of. But these were manageable things.

I would suggest a meeting place that had the potential, through an accident of design (much as I felt myself to be), to shield me from any risky revisiting of his wife's spectacular ground floor. Along with absorption in matters related to how the gods had assembled Bob's wife, I enjoyed an esthetic pleasure of close to equal force when allowing my eyes to linger over old-school Italian espresso machines, which made the Cafe Trieste a natural choice for our rendezvous. It would be my treat. I'd get there ahead of time, station myself at a table close to the door, keep an eye on approaching customers. When catching sight of Bob and his wife, I'd turn toward the espresso machine. They'd say my name, naturally expecting my head to turn toward them. "Sit down," I'd say, "I'm in a trance." Certainly they might find such a response odd, but once Bob's wife was seated and her ankles safely tucked under the table, I would turn and explain. They would be fascinated as I outlined how an occasional trance-like state overcame me in response to the beautiful workmanship that went into the very best espresso machines. "So glad you guys could make it," I'd go on to say in the casual, friendly way you speak to people with whom you harbor no secret obsessions. I dispatched my second letter with great confidence.

Bob did not reply.

After a year or so, I was starting to think I would never hear back from Bob. It was unbearable. I couldn't concentrate. I barely slept. I was falling behind on every task. My boss wanted to speak to me about my work performance. I sent a third letter confessing that the imposter letter was a ruse; that I was the imposter. Yes, Bob, I admitted, the imposter was the imposter. I nursed the hope that Bob's compassion would be aroused with the same vigor that I had found myself aroused by his wife's ankles, that his heart would open as he began to comprehend the scale of my distress, the lengths I was willing to go to in order to make amends, and that perhaps now he would understand the incalculable enormity of my admiration for his wife's you-know-whats as well as the intensity of my wish to take back my enthusiastic but out-of-place expression in regard to them.

I thought there was a good chance Bob would write me back, given how thoroughly I had laid bare my soul.

As of this writing, there has been no word yet from Bob.

# DINNER

ALL THE GUESTS WERE couples. I was the lone single. I told myself not to think of it as deeply symbolic. I told myself it might have been a coincidence or maybe an act of compassion on the part of the couples. I told myself it would be over soon. Like life itself, it would not go on forever. Even when I had been doubled, I'd felt single. I didn't understand why. When I'd said to my partner, Cathy, that I felt single, she said, "Well, fuck off then," which kind of confirmed my feelings. People say it's good to have a partner who confirms your feelings, but in that case it wasn't so good. The host of the dinner party had not told me that it would be a couples party so maybe he didn't see it that way. Maybe he had an enlightened view and saw it simply as a people party, and by virtue of me being a person I was includable. It's good to be includable, but you never know how long it's going to last. And I still felt like the sole exception to something, which detracted from any momentary joy associated with feelings of inclusion. I hate when I have a moment of joy and then a thought comes along to detract from it. But it always happens. I wondered if the coupled people who sat around the table from me also felt, on occasion at any rate, like sole exceptions of a sort and made up for the ensuing discomfort by snuggling up with another sole exception in a shared bed at the end of the day. I felt like it was a fair enough theory, but I didn't feel comfortable testing out my theory with a question because it simply wasn't the sort of question it felt wise to pose as the one single person in a sea of couples. What I have noticed is the good questions often have to be shelved or saved for another time, a time that never comes. Unless of course there was to come a time when I myself might share a bed with another person. But by then it might be too late, at least too late to pose an honest question or get an honest answer, one that would lend some integrity to the research. If you want to maintain your integrity, a shared bed can pose unforeseen challenges.

Two large bowls of noodles slathered in meat sauce were passed around. This was a cultured crowd, and the food, which came without a salad or really vegetables of any kind, seemed orgiastic and out of place. That consoled me since an out-of-place feeling was one I felt a special kinship with. A very drunk woman sat across from me, which I have never really objected to. As a rule I rather like it at first, then later not as much. She placed a tremendous pile of noodles on her plate. I loved the lusty way she did it. This is food, I'm having some, was the kind of style in which she went about accomplishing it. I was starting to admire this drunken woman who told me her name was Sandra. I had not asked her her name. Between mouthfuls, she just came right out and gave it to me. Fair enough, I thought, and most sociable. I think she knew things, like how the real questions seldom get asked. And she probably could tell that I was an appreciator of her appreciations, her relationship to the noodles being one obvious example.

I felt sure she sensed my growing admiration.

In this way she was her own type of sole exception— exceptionally attuned to a particular type of admirer. She let me know that she was an artist who specialized in installations and said she could place me in one of her installations because her intuition led her to believe

I'd be very installable. I was ready to have her stick me any old place she wanted. She had formidable teeth, which was not something that worried me, and also a stain on her white blouse that did worry me. I wanted the power not to fall under the spell of that stain, which had become, in terms of impression, as significant as the person wearing it, if that's the proper way to speak of a stain, as something worn. I made efforts to look away but was continuously drawn back. I wanted to alert her to it, but its location made that feel too daring because, as everyone, particularly her partner, would surely know, her breasts were inside that blouse. It was really the only place her breasts could be. I wished that the stain had been on her sleeve because a stain on her sleeve would have led me to point out its exact and fortuitously innocuous location. That would have been perfectly appropriate and even useful, and I had this theory that women appreciate men who were useful. But a stain shows up where it wants to, and that's life, as Frank Sinatra once sang, and a great many other people have come to much the same conclusion.

# FEAR OF POETS

**YOU MADE A DASH** for it. It wasn't too late. You get to literary events early, which may be bad for your nervous system. Most of the choices you make seem to be bad for your nervous system. It was a poetry reading you were waiting patiently for. Who in their right mind does that? It's like kicking back and taking in the view before the firing squad points its rifles in your direction. The poets all showed up, of course, seeing as how they like to gang up on you. You'd think at least one of them could have stayed home with a cold. Not a chance. In they marched. You trembled in a corner. They took their seats in a fashion only poets can. You'd hardly call it sitting down. You'd describe it, but your sentences could never live up to their soaring, incomprehensible lyric. They were seated in front of you, obscuring any chance you may have had of a reasonable view. And, of course, breathing their fiery hot breath on your neck from right behind you. How sobering it is to be encircled by such an intimidating mob. Try as you might, you won't get comfortable around such people. Why, they mutter away quite without a trace of formalism and will pick a fight with you on the spot should you point out the irony of the situation. Press your ear to the atmosphere of their conversing and it is totally missing any of those strategic repeating lines they salivate over. You wave at them in order to suggest the possibility of connection, although you are not sure what you would do if you achieved it. How would you ever live up to inclusion in such august company? And really, is it connection you're after, or are you just hedging your bets, making a preemptive move in the direction of self-defense? An insurance policy to protect you from the ardent fire of the poet's wrath. Quite wrathful buggers they are, too, despite all that flowery language. But not to worry about your wave that went unacknowledged. Being poets, they either pretend not to see you or are caught up in some interior reverie you will later be subjected to the result of when you dutifully pop down your twelve bucks for their chapbook. Chapbook, yes, which you only recently realized is all one word, not two. You'll be keeping that to yourself, especially when surrounded by the fearsome poets. You'd think they'd notice your fraught and frightened condition and give you a break. A line break, maybe, not much else. The sad part is none of these signs, which don't exactly require bifocals to notice, curtail your impulse to inject yourself into their bubbling stream of consciousness or whatever the hell it is they are wafting around in. Your need is as palpable as it is unexplainable.

Well, that's poetry for you.

# AUTHOR

**"I LOVE HOW YOU** do that," she said.

I was flossing my teeth at the time. I felt the warm glow of her admiration. You know what that can do. I got the idea I could teach her things, be the well from which she might quench her thirst. Her long, shapely leg rested on the rim of my bathtub. I thought to myself, that's my bathtub, that's her leg.

"What should we do now?" she asked in a seductive tone.

"I could read you a section from my novel," I said, immediately regretting it, immediately sensing how such an answer turns your life to shit.

"What's it about?" she said, the light going out of her eyes, her leg leaving the rim of my bathtub. I plunged ahead, thinking who knows what, that I might, through well-formulated self- expression, win back her former good feelings for me.

"Well, it involves a young man who, shall we say, aspires to be other than he presently is, who wants his life to register as actual, as in ..."

"I don't get it," she said, interrupting and reaching in her pocket for some gum. "It's later than I thought," she added, checking her phone. I wanted to beg, say, "Please don't leave. It's only nine-thirty and I am not really a guy who wants to talk about a stupid book. I'm a guy who wants your leg back resting on the rim of my bathtub, a guy who wants to be admired for the way I thread that fine cord through my teeth. And I was just warming up; there are many other aspects of personal hygiene I'd like to demonstrate for you."

I never got to say it. The door slammed shut. The click-clacking sound of her heels got fainter and fainter out in the hallway.

## LOVERS

**I HAVE HAD LOVERS**, I'm happy to say, although I don't know why I say it like that. Maybe I think of it as a figure of speech, or there's a curvaceous figure acting up in the basement of my subconscious, the lower basement, since the whole subconscious is one big-ass basement to begin with. Or I'm just letting it roll off my tongue without thinking it through when I should be holding my tongue, or not even introducing the subject of my tongue while I am in fact wagging the very tongue to which I refer. If I had simply said I have had lovers, that has about it a forthrightness that, when it comes to speaking of lovers, may be too forthright. But now, given a chance to look back on it—not looking back on the lovers, although one is always looking back on them, isn't one, trying to discern the meaning of those markers in one's life, those intervals of time, fleeting triumphs, lapses of judgement, gathering them all up in an unruly, haphazard basket, unless one had a neat basket with lovers of a tidy, orderly variety, perhaps a whole well-managed queue of past lovers taking their turn—but their turn to do what, you ask. Well, that's a provocative question and I am no expert on the desires of others, their various itches, their mysterious urges, their propensities, their proclivities, their patent-leather shoes. I can hardly keep my own straight, but I imagine each of them would probably want to do something different, or do something similar, or maybe a creative melding of similar and different to kind of cover the waterfront, because a lover who covers the waterfront throws down a formidable anchor.

And you may wish to be tethered to just such a vessel.

But I can't speak with any kind of authority, not even port authority, on account of never having had a basket like that. So rather than look back upon the lovers or collect an inventory of their proposals—rather than that, which might require extensive research, audience participation, a general survey, or feedback forms, which I neglected to bring along—rather than that, let's revisit the first sentence of this piece, the addition of "I'm happy to say" to the more concise statement of "I have had lovers." "I'm happy to say" has a suspect tone, an almost repulsive glibness, and one should never be glib and certainly not repulsive when it comes to speaking of lovers. Not that it was meant as an expression of confidence, but was really more an expression of gratitude. But even the sentence "I have had lovers, I'm grateful to say" contains a type of swagger, placing oneself as it does in a superior position to those who have not had lovers or have had but one. But as Ronald Reagan was said to have remarked in regard to the redwoods, if you have had one, you've had them all. Well, he probably said seen, but it starts often enough with seeing, does it not? Although we might all be better served if it started on parchment or through an audio device of some kind. Heaven knows there's enough of those around these days. And don't think I don't know that you hear the lament of the aging in that last observation, which brings to mind the times in which we live and love, our current-day lovers, as in cutting-edge lovers, lovers who have invested in all the most modern equipment, whose drawers are full to bursting with the latest bells and whistles, who are themselves, in their lovemaking skills, bells and whistles of an outstanding caliber. Yes, lovers who are both up-to-date and current, and therefore not surprisingly but very much currently engaged in lovemaking. Maybe not right this minute, but at more or less regular intervals during the course of their lovership. Yes, it brings to mind this business of present-day lovers looking over their shoulders at the lovers who preceded the ones with whom they are now engaged. Which inevitably raises the how many question and regrettably returns us to the opening sentence of this piece: "I have had lovers." A bit of a cul-de-sac, isn't it, but we can claw our way out. Not that the mention of claws should hint at a propensity for lovemaking that leaves its mark, marking as it might the tender flesh of the object of our affection who is not, of course, an object, not a toy train or something like that, more like a redwood, actually, a vibrant, incomprehensible life form cavorting with another incomprehensible life form, or one incomprehensible life form after another, or even several at once, which, although pleasantly invitational and admirably inclusive, from my present perspective just might be overdoing it a little.

# INCIDENT

**"DID YOU SEE THAT** man? I think he was coming on to you. It looked very intrusive."

"What man?"

"The one who bumped into you, or pretended to bump into you."

"This is a bustling drugstore. We live in San Francisco. There's not a lot of room, what with the number of people and all."

"That's very tolerant. I admire your attitude. But I think his behavior was inappropriate, and not in any way accidental."

"Whose behavior?"

"The man, the one you are giving the benefit of the doubt to, the one whose behavior you ascribe to congestion."

"Well, that's where you've got me stumped. I just don't know which man you're referring to, or what exactly he did. Although I'm becoming interested."

"Interested? How do you mean?"

"I guess I'm interested in the man you noticed."

"In what way?"

"Well, could you start with a description?"

"What type of description?"

"For instance, what did he look like?"

"He was portly."

"Was he indeed? I have to say I've never been one of those women who rules out a man just on account of a little extra weight."

"Given his size, it's even more baffling that you remained unaware of his obnoxious behavior."

"Well, my eyes have never been good."

"I suppose I have to let the whole thing pass, particularly since you are not upset."

"Yes, it hardly seems worth wasting energy on, but I would appreciate it if you backed up a bit. After all, we are just strangers talking, and your body language is starting to feel rather intimate."

"Gosh, sorry, I thought I was a good three feet away."

"Perhaps you possess a type of dynamism that makes you feel closer than you actually are."

"Do you think so?"

"Entirely possible. And I'm a bit of an expert."

"On what?"

"Male energy."

"There he is, the man who bumped into you. He's over by the tortilla chips."

"Oh, him. That's Arthur, my husband. We just got hitched this morning down at City Hall."

"Your husband. Oh, I'm terribly sorry."

"Don't be. I'm quite happy with him so far, although it hasn't been long."

"When he appeared to bump into you, I didn't see any sign that you knew him."

"Well, I don't know him all that well."

"He seemed like a total stranger."

"Yes, that's precisely what I look for in a husband, which may explain the number of times I've gone the bride route. Arthur, bless his heart, is number nine."

"You don't look old enough."

"Thank you. We seem to be getting on better now, don't you think? At first I thought you might be a sort of extremist out to put an end to accidental contact."

"I sincerely regret giving such an impression."

"Do you mind if I ask you a question?"

"Go ahead."

"Be honest, what do you think the chances are for me and Arthur?"

"So difficult to say. I don't know you two well enough."

"Because, to be frank, I'm beginning to worry about where we're headed."

"You and Arthur?"

"No, not at all, you and I."

"You mean the two of us?"

"Yes, because I'm now quite sure you possess that male dynamism I mentioned."

"Really?"

"Yes, and here's the thing, I'm never wrong."

"I have to admit to being flattered. And even though it seems improper to say, particularly under the circumstances, you being freshly wed and so forth, I'm quite aroused."

"Well, why don't you come a little closer? There's no way to explore this type of thing with you all the way over there."

# ROOM

I GOT ALL COMFY listening to the poets, and the introduction of the poets, and the room the poets were in, and the armchairs which held the poets' bottoms and made rested the poets' elbows, the poets' arms, and the poets who were there to listen to the poets. And then I thought, oh, we will never die, because I didn't have to be realistic. I wasn't compelled to face facts. I was with the poets and they were with me. And the temperature was unruly, unpredictable. The weather went through a great deal in the room that held the poets. And I remained comfy. Two women were the poets who lounged and read. Yes, there were two. And many were the others, and I was one. When the sound was not quite right, when the mic was too far or too close, it was as though nothing went wrong, like the wild weather changes made nothing go wrong. They were just wild weather changes, if you know what I mean. Both the poets were beautiful, and the introducer of the poets was beautiful, and all of us gathered there were beautiful and we couldn't help it. One of the poets had the flouncy style. And I loved the soft flounce of it that didn't billow over and bury us beneath. The other had zippers and some leather patches but still managed to possess a flouncy quality. And it was sheer poetry, which is a way I knew that only our bodies would die. The rest would be alive still, the other parts that no name was good for. And then, while still in the body, I noticed the bodies of the poets that were in front of us. With great courage those bodies were there, and still nothing was wrong. I caught sight of the place where the breast begins on one of the poets, just the beginning, not the exclamatory cleavage of a tumultuous ocean, just a tributary, a small start, so subtle and lovely. And I thought, as I am thinking now, don't add too many words. For she is here for a short time. And I held the bunch of thank you in me, and I didn't linger.

## ACKNOWLEDGEMENTS

First and foremost, thank you to my wife, Alison. There would not have been one paragraph without her. And to my writing teachers: Mary Webb, Elizabeth Rosner, Tamam Kahn, Genine Lentine, Jamey Genna, and Joshua Mohr.

To J. K. Fowler for believing my work warranted the form of a book.

To Evan Karp and everyone at Quiet Lightning.

And to Matthew James DeCoster for valued and cherished early support.

Many additional thanks to the journals in which some of these stories first appeared: *sPARKLE & bLINK*: "Admiration,""Author," "Dinner," "Hearth and Home," "Poetry," "Take Two," "The Reading," "Unglued," "Unwise," and "Who?"; *eleven eleven*, issue 19: "A Date"; *The Oakland Review*, #3: "Lovers"; and *Sweet Wolverine*: "Mixed Formula."

**PETER THOMAS BULLEN**, a hairdresser and co-founder of Peter Thomas Hair in Berkeley, California, began writing at the urging of his wife. After throwing himself blindly into the literary open mic scene, he discovered that if you are standing at the front of a room holding text and trembling slightly, people will give you their attention. Sometimes they will even say something kind to you. This made him happy.

He was a Quiet Lightning Neighborhood Hero in 2014, and has twice been a featured reader at San Francisco's LitQuake. His work has appeared in *sPARKLE & bLINK*, *eleven eleven*, *The Oakland Review*, *Blotterature*, *Sweet Wolverine*, and the *Los Angeles Review of Books*. He blogs at wetriedourbest. wordpress.com.